For Nancy ~ S. S.

For Princess Lenora Wendy
Coco Bell (aka Nora) ~ C. P.

**tiger tales**
5 River Road, Suite 128, Wilton, CT 06897
Published in the United States 2022
Originally published in Great Britain 2022
by Little Tiger Press Ltd.
Text copyright © 2022 Suzy Senior
Illustrations copyright © 2022 Claire Powell
ISBN-13: 978-1-68010-284-0
ISBN-10: 1-68010-284-2
Printed in China
LTP/2800/4395/0222
All rights reserved
2 4 6 8 10 9 7 5 3 1

www.tigertalesbooks.com

# WHO WILL KISS the CROCODILE?

by SUZY SENIOR

Illustrated by CLAIRE POWELL

tiger tales

When Princess Liss was one year old,
her family threw a ball —

*a great big fancy party*

in the castle's grandest hall.

The guests dug out their nicest clothes;
the town was so excited.

But someone was not on the list.
She **NEVER** got **INVITED!**

The party was amazing!
    There was dancing, fun, and laughter,
piles of fancy sandwiches,
    and sweets and treats served after.

But suddenly, the hall went cold.
The candles flickered out.
The doors flew off their hinges,
and there came a wicked shout:

"I see that you've forgotten ME!
Well, here's my gift:

# SURPRISE!

In fifteen years, she'll bump her knee.
And then the princess **DIES!**"

The angry fairy waved her wand
and added with a hiss:
"And just for fun, until that day,
the girl will look like this . . . !"

The King went pale. He clutched his beard
and gave a little **YELP.**
"My darling daughter!" sobbed the Queen.
"Can anybody help?"

"I can!" a nearby fairy cried.
"I'll save our Princess Liss!
She will NOT die! She'll sleep until
she's woken with a kiss."

"Well, thanks for that!" the King declared.
He gave a nervous smile.
"The kiss part might be tricky, though.
Who will kiss a **CROCODILE?**"

The years went by — the Princess grew;
her teeth were sharp and strong.
Her skin turned tough and scaly,
and her claws were fiercely long.

On the day she turned sixteen,
she went swimming in the lake.
She hit a rock and bumped her knee —
**OH, NO!** A big mistake!

Back home, she bandaged up her knee.
It really did look bruised!
She went to bed to take a nap, and snoozed

*and snoozed . . .*

*and snoozed!*

The castle stood, enchanted;
  the hedge grew thick and black.
And deep inside, a fair princess
  lay snoring on her back.

The princes came from miles around
to do their princely duty:
  - Wake the princess
  - Claim the kingdom
  - Marry Sleeping Beauty

They brought their swords and kissy lips . . .
but then they ran a mile!
The fearless princes wouldn't dare
to kiss a **CROCODILE!**

As time went on,
the hedge grew **WILD;**
    the mighty turrets crumbled.
    "We'll have to find a handyman!"
      the worried neighbors grumbled.

Would **ANYONE** be brave enough?
The word spread far and wide . . . .
Until one day, a van screeched up
with writing on the side:

For BUILDING WORK and GARDEN JOBS,
and CLEANING CEILINGS, too,
call Clare and Katarina NOW and HIRE
the FIX-IT CREW!

They started work at 8 a.m. and barely stopped all day.

They **HAMMERED, DRILLED,**

and **MOPPED,**

then **CUT** the thorny hedge away.

As evening fell, they found her,
with her knee still sore and red:
A **FEARSOME**-looking **CROCODILE!**
Just fast asleep in bed!

The Fix-it Crew is pretty **TOUGH**;
they didn't **RUN** and **SCREAM.**
The only place they ran to was
their van to get some cream.

"This cream is something special.
Works like *magic*," whispered Clare.
She rubbed it gently on the knee.
"That ought to fix it. There!"

"We'll be back soon. Sweet dreams for now,"
called Clare to sleeping Liss.
**"Good night,"** said Katarina,
and she blew a little . . .

. . . kiss!

**"OH, MY!"** cried Katarina.
**"OOH!** What happened here?" said Clare.

**"*Good morning,*"** yawned the Princess
with a grin and bed-head hair.

The castle **CREAKED** and slowly stirred,
   awakened from the spell.
Liss rushed to hug her mom and dad
   (they'd been asleep as well).

The next weekend, to celebrate,
the Princess held a ball —

*a great big fancy party*

in the castle's grandest hall.

The guests dug out their nicest clothes.
The town was so excited.
(And Liss made very sure that
**EVERYBODY** was invited.)

The Fix-it Crew was honored —
no more cleaning up today!
They put their sparkly dresses on
and danced the night away.

The party was amazing!
There was feasting, fun, and laughter,
and — yes, you might have guessed —
they all lived

**HAPPILY EVER AFTER.**